W9-CPY-496

OSCAR OTTER

An I Can Read Book®

OSCAR OTTER

BY NATHANIEL BENCHLEY
Illustrations by Arnold Lobel

HarperTrophy®
A Division of HarperCollins*Publishers*

OSCAR OTTER
Text copyright © 1966 by Nathaniel G. Benchley
Text copyright renewed 1994 by Marjorie Benchley
Pictures copyright © 1966 by Arnold Lobel
Pictures copyright renewed 1994 by Adam Lobel

Library of Congress Catalog Card Number: 66-11499
ISBN 0-06-020472-9 (lib. bdg.)
ISBN 0-06-444025-7 (pbk.)

First Harper Trophy edition, 1980.

Oscar was a young otter.

He lived by the side of a pond.

With the other otters,

he would often play

on the otter slide,

6

coming down the bank

with a great rush, going

SPLASH!

into the water.

One day,

when he was on the slide alone,

he came to a corner and

SMACK! He ran right into a tree.

"What's the big idea?"

Oscar asked the beaver.

"That tree is in my way."

"Sorry," said the beaver,

"but winter's coming,

and I have to build a house."

He began to chew down another tree.

Oscar told his father

what had happened.

"So build another slide,"

said his father,

14

his mouth full of fish.

"There are lots of places."

"All right, I will," said Oscar.

"I'll show that beaver.

I'll build a slide

that goes way up

into their mountains, there."

"I wouldn't do that,"

his father replied.

"You'll get too far

from the water."

"Who needs water?" said Oscar.

"*You* need water," his father said.

"Other animals will catch you

if you go too far away."

But Oscar didn't listen.

He began to build a secret slide.

"I won't tell anyone," he said.

"Then no one can catch me."

He built it up

and up

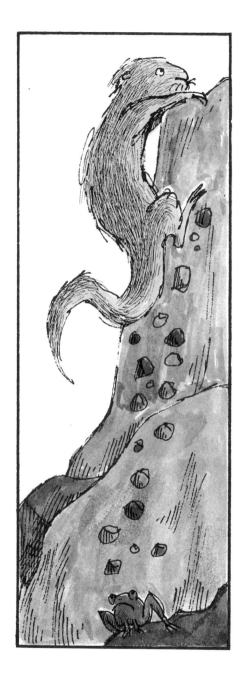

through the woods

and into the mountain.

It took a long time.

At the end of each day

he would come down the slide.

When, at last,

he had built his slide

as far as it would go,

26

he looked around

and saw the land below him,

spread over like a map.

27

"This looks interesting," he said.

"I think I'll explore."

28

He started off

down the mountain.

And pretty soon he was lost.

All the trees looked alike.

He couldn't tell where he had come from.

Then he had a bright idea.

"I came *down* the hill," he said.

"So if I go *up* the hill again,

I'll find my slide."

He started up the hill. But . . .

there was something he didn't know.

He was being watched by a fox

who, in his turn,

was being watched by a wolf

who was being watched by

a mountain lion

who, if you can believe it,

was being watched by a moose

38

who thought he was in

a circus parade.

The moose gave a moose call,

to see if there was

another moose in the parade.

HONK!

This made all the other animals jump.

The fox jumped at Oscar!

The wolf jumped at the fox!

And the mountain lion

leaped at the wolf!

But Oscar

had found

his slide

and he jumped

onto it,

followed by

all the others,

except the moose,

who thought they were crazy,

and walked away.

51

As Oscar came near the pond

there was a sharp turn

and another tree

that the beaver had cut down!

"Help!" cried Oscar.

"Please help me!"

Quick as a flash,

the beaver made a ramp with his tail

and Oscar zoomed over.

The beaver hurried off.

The others crashed into the tree,

but Oscar landed safely in the pond.

"You're late for supper,"

his father said.

"Where have you been?"

"Late?" said Oscar.

"I almost *was* supper—a fox's supper."

"Next time," said his father,

"will we try to be not quite so smart?"

"What next time?" replied Oscar.

"I am happy right here where I am."